little Miss Brainy

by Roger Hargreaves

WORLD INTERNATIONAL

Little Miss Brainy was very brainy.

She knew an awful lot of things.

She knew simple things such as
if you want a good night's sleep you
have to go to bed.

And, if you want to get up,
then first, you have to wake up.

She knew that if you don't want to be hungry,
you have to eat.

Little Miss Brainy
also knew lots of very clever things.

She knew that it is quite impossible
for centipedes to find matching coloured
shoes for **all** their feet.

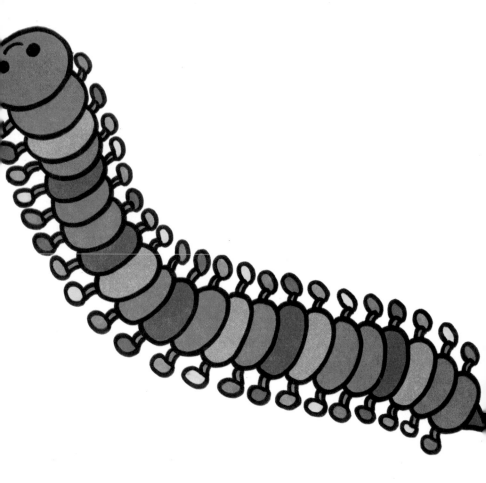

Now, Little Miss Brainy knew so much
that people got to hear about it.

They came from far and wide
to ask her questions.

Mr Messy called to see her.

"What can I do to keep myself messy?"
he asked.

"I know!" cried Little Miss Brainy.
"Don't wash!"

Mr Messy was delighted.

As Mr Messy was leaving, Mr Dizzy arrived.

"Is there anything heavier than a hippopotamus?"
asked Mr Dizzy.

"I know!" said Little Miss Brainy.
"Two hippopotamuses!"

"Is that so?" said Mr Dizzy.
"I'll go and check."

Mr Clever arrived.
"What colour is my green hat?" he asked.

"I know!" sighed Little Miss Brainy,
nodding her head.
"It's green, of course!"

"Oh, you know so many clever things!"
exclaimed Mr Clever.

Mr Clever left,
and so did Little Miss Brainy.

She had had enough of listening to
such simple questions.

So she travelled to a place called Cleverland,
where she hoped that everybody would ask
her some difficult questions for a change.

When she got there, she stopped
in front of a tree.

There was a pig sitting on one of its branches.

"However am I going to get down from here?"
wailed the pig.

"I know!" said Little Miss Brainy.
"You can jump down!"

"Good idea," said the pig,
and being a Cleverland pig he jumped …
right on top of Little Miss Brainy.

"You're not as soft as a pillow,"
he complained, and he trotted off.

Further down the road
Little Miss Brainy met an elephant.

He had a knot tied in his trunk.

"Please 'elp be. How cad I ud-do dis
dot id by trunk?" he asked, in a funny
sort of way.

"I know," said Little Miss Brainy.
"I'll undo it for you."

And she did.

"Phew!" gasped the elephant.

And blew Little Miss Brainy high into the air!

"I feel much better now," said the elephant.

"I don't!" moaned Little Miss Brainy,
and rubbed her head.

The elephant had blown her some
distance away and she landed in front of a …

… lion!

"I'm starving!" growled the lion.
"What can I eat?"

Little Miss Brainy looked around,
but she could see nothing,
and said quickly …

"I don't know!"

And she ran home,
before the lion realised
that she was the only
thing to eat for miles around!